EXPLORING ROMAN MYTHOLOGY

Don Nardo

San Diego, CA

© 2025 ReferencePoint Press, Inc.
Printed in the United States

For more information, contact:
ReferencePoint Press, Inc.
PO Box 27779
San Diego, CA 92198
www.ReferencePointPress.com

LIBRARY OF CONGRESS CATALOGING-IN-PUBLICATION DATA

Names: Nardo, Don, 1947- author.
Title: Exploring Roman mythology / by Don Nardo.
Description: San Diego, CA : ReferencePoint Press, Inc., [2025] | Includes
    bibliographical references and index.
Identifiers: LCCN 2023048420 (print) | LCCN 2023048421 (ebook) | ISBN
    9781678207823 (library binding) | ISBN 9781678207830 (ebook)
Subjects: LCSH: Mythology, Roman--Juvenile literature. |
    Rome--Religion--Juvenile literature.
Classification: LCC BL803 .N367 2025 (print) | LCC BL803 (ebook) | DDC
    292.1/3--dc23/eng/20231101
LC record available at https://lccn.loc.gov/2023048420
LC ebook record available at https://lccn.loc.gov/2023048421

CONTENTS

A City Destined to Rule the World?

Long ago, a small convoy of sailing ships approached the shores of western Italy, somewhat south of where Rome would be established several generations later. The leader of the squadron, a young man named Aeneas, had been a prince of Troy, located hundreds of miles to the east. When that city had fallen to a Greek army, Aeneas and his followers had escaped and, acting on a prophecy from a god, had embarked on a grueling, dangerous journey to Italy. There, the prophecy had claimed, Aeneas would establish a family line that would lead to the creation of a highly successful future city.

Aeneas ordered a landing at Cumae, not far north of present-day Naples, and immediately tracked down the Sibyl. Mentioned in the prophecy, she was a mysterious woman who, it was said, had the ability to see future events. Wearing a long black robe, she welcomed Aeneas. He must travel further north to the fertile plain of Latium, she told him, for that was where he was fated to establish himself as the father of a new and noble people.

After thanking the Sibyl for her advice, he asked her for a favor. Could she show him a way to reach the underworld? His father, Anchises, had recently died, he explained, and he yearned to see the older man one last time.

Fortunately for Aeneas, the woman's response was positive. She led him down a dark, winding path until they arrived at the outer edge of the realm of the dead. There, Aeneas found and greeted his father. And old Anchises conjured up a brief, partial vision of the noble race Aeneas would soon establish. "I shall show you the whole span of our destiny," Anchises said. In Latium, some of Aeneas's descendants would give rise to an individual named Romulus—who would build a city called Rome. Anchises added, "Our glorious Rome shall rule the whole wide world, and her spirit shall match the spirit of the gods."[1]

Aeneas's father also revealed short visions of a few of the numerous Roman heroes and leaders who were destined to make Rome great. That array of righteous individuals, Anchises went on, would reach its pinnacle in the greatest of them all—Augustus Caesar. Anchises described Augustus as "a child of the Divine"—a ruler who would initiate "a golden age"[2] for Rome and the world.

Virgil, Augustus, and the National Epic

These words supposedly spoken by Aeneas's father come from Rome's massive and magnificent national epic poem, the 9,896-line *Aeneid*. It was penned in the late first century BCE by one of Rome finest writers, Virgil. His reference to his close friend Augustus, then Rome's most powerful person, was no accident. Following a long period of destructive civil wars that had recently brought the Roman government to its knees, a single figure emerged the victor. His name was Octavian. Intimidated by the vast power the young man now wielded, the Roman Senate conferred upon him the title of Augustus, "the revered one." And he rapidly transformed Rome's government into an autocracy—the Roman Empire—which would endure for some five centuries. Virgil's creation of the new national epic was meant in large part to be a tribute to the founding of this momentous new Roman order.

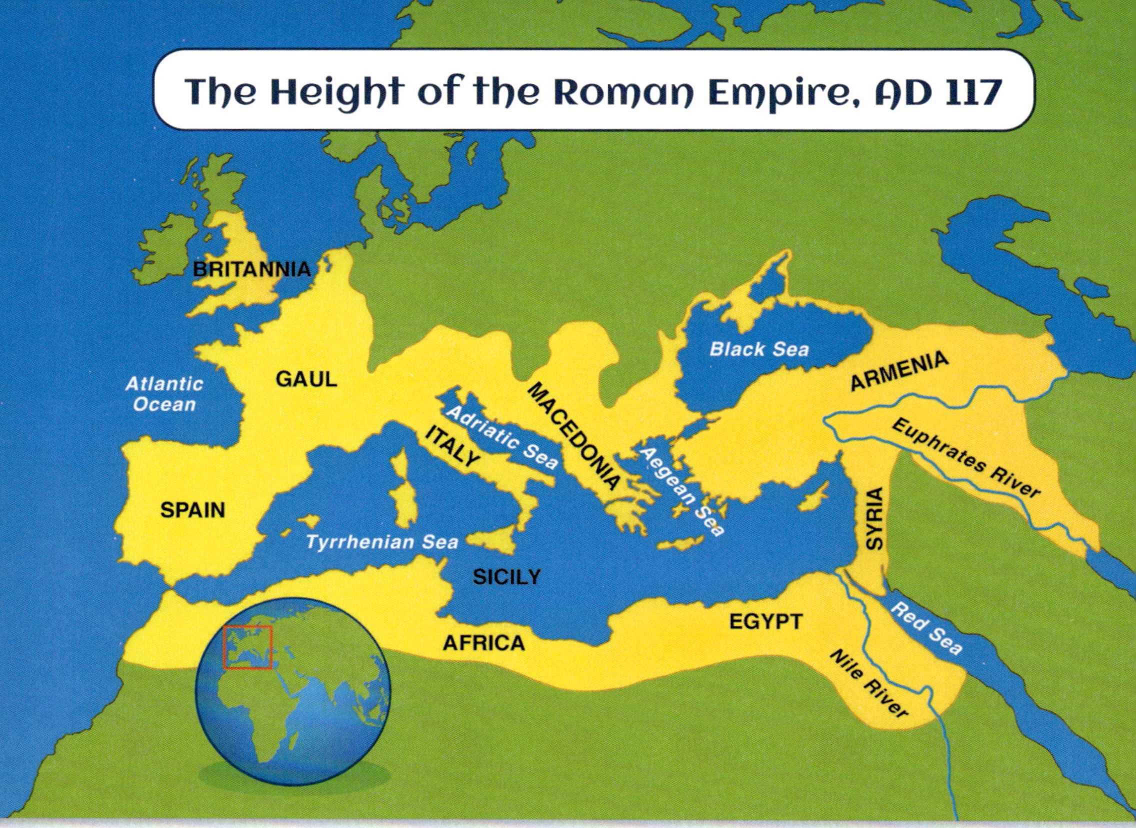

In addition to glorifying Augustus and the new Rome, Virgil's other motivation for writing the *Aeneid* was to provide Rome with important additions to its national mythology. There were already a number of national heroes of the past whom the Romans held in awe, Aeneas and Romulus among them. But Virgil greatly expanded Aeneas's story, adding many new mythical episodes to the mix. Another great writer of the Augustan period, the historian Livy, did the same by adding much detail to Romulus's already existing tales of old.

To the Roman people, this vast compendium of old and new myths was not simply diverting and entertaining, as the Greek and Roman myths are to people today. Rather, the Romans believed that the people and events of those stories had been real as well as sanctioned and guided by the gods. Indeed, according to Virgil, the chief Roman deity, Jupiter, had proclaimed that Rome would be supreme among nations for all times. This was only right, the god said, because the Romans were the world's worthiest people. Livy also echoed this idea in the introduction to his mammoth history of Rome, saying, "If any nation deserves the privilege of claiming a divine ancestry, that nation is our own. And so great is the glory won by the Roman people . . . that when they declare that Mars [god of war] himself was their first parent and father of the man who founded their city, all the nations of the world [must readily agree]."[3]

Creating the Roman Lake

Whether or not the gods ordained Rome's rise to greatness, the fact is that Rome eventually came to create a vast and powerful empire. Beginning as a small, crude farming community in about 1000 BCE, it slowly grew into one of western Italy's strongest city-states. In ca. 509 BCE, the Romans established the Roman Republic, with a semi-democratic government run by a senate and various elected officials. The Republic then rapidly expanded until it controlled all of Italy.

Moving outward into the Mediterranean, the Romans gained control of most of the lands bordering the western sector of that waterway by 201 BCE. Then they conquered the Greek lands of the sea's eastern sector. By the time of the civil wars in the 100s BCE, the Mediterranean was in essence a Roman lake (as Rome controlled all the lands along its shores). And after Augustus's creation of the empire, Rome came to control even more sections of Europe and much of the Middle East as well.

In all, Roman civilization lasted well over fourteen centuries. Throughout that long period, the myths from its early years—about divinely guided, patriotic heroes—continued to pass from generation to generation. "Every Roman schoolboy was taught" the legends of Rome's formative centuries, noted scholar Jane F. Gardner explains. Those tales "exemplified the virtues that the Romans liked to think were part of the essential [and stalwart] Roman character." In this way, "the Romans [defined] themselves through the stories they [told] about their past—that is, through their myths."[4]

CHAPTER ONE

Rome's Many Borrowed Gods and Myths

The ancient Romans long perpetuated a colorful tale from their remote past, back in the dimly remembered period when Rome was first established. At one point, the story goes, several Roman men abducted women from a neighboring people—the Sabines—hoping to make them Roman wives. In response, a small army of well-armed Sabine soldiers attacked Rome, their mission to retrieve the women at any cost.

What the invaders did not plan for was that at least some of the gods the Romans worshipped might come to the town's defense. In this case only a single deity intervened; but his efforts proved crucial to Rome's continuing survival. Called Janus, he was the god of doorways and gates, beginnings and endings, and the ongoing transition of time from day to day and year to year. He also oversaw the start and finish of conflicts; in Roman eyes, that meant that he inspired Rome's leaders to either make war or declare peace.

Unlike the gods of ancient Greece, Janus had no physical body, so he could not fight the invaders by laying hands on them. But that did not mean he lacked the ability to help the people who worshipped him. When the Sabine soldiers were about to pass through a gate that led to the Forum—the main town square—Janus saw a golden opportunity. As the god of gates and other doorways, his divine magic was greatest at the moment that people or objects passed through those portals. That, he reasoned, would allow him to make the attackers pay dearly. According to the first-century-BCE Roman poet Ovid, Janus himself later recalled:

> Now the foe had reached the gate, [to stop them] I slyly had recourse to a device of my own craft. . . . I opened the fountains' mouths [positioned over a hot spring] and spouted out a sudden gush of water; but first I threw sulphur into the water channels, that the boiling liquid might bar the way against [the enemy]. This service done, and the Sabines repulsed, the [city was] now rendered safe [and] resumed its former aspect.[5]

To thank Janus for his help, the Romans installed an outdoor altar in the Forum. There people regularly sacrificed animals and plants in his honor. Moreover, that shrine later expanded into a full-fledged temple dedicated to him.

Rome's Initial, Simplistic Deities

Janus's tale in which he repelled an invading force of Sabines was unusual in the annals of early Roman mythology. This is because he was one of only a handful of the Roman deities of that era who had any myths at all. During that formative period—roughly spanning 1000 to 500 BCE—Rome was still a small farming community in western Italy. It had little in the way of lands or political and military influence. And at the time, the gods the residents of that modest town worshipped had very few personal background stories attached to them. Most had none at all, which made Janus stand out.

The main reason for this dearth of early Roman myths about the gods is the way the Romans initially saw those beings. Before Rome came into close contact with the Greek city-states and kingdoms in the last four centuries BCE, the Romans worshipped a group of deities called numina. These entities were viewed as very simplistic and largely formless nature spirits. Each possessed one or two mostly small-scale functions or duties and oversaw only a small, very limited aspect of life. Janus was an example. The late historian R.M. Ogilvie explained how the Romans saw him and other numina as having very basic, localized functions:

> Most of the things which were vital for the well-being of society were thought of as functions of a god or as gods functioning. A house is only as secure as its door. The opening and closing of the door, and the passage of a person from the privacy of the home into the racket of the outside world, and *vice versa*, can be critical events, and, in consequence, they were held to be in the power of a god: Janus.[6]

Hundreds of other numina, each with their own particular power, were thought to inhabit the world. The numen Sylvanus had the specific duty of protecting woodcutters. And Concordia did nothing else but oversee contracts and other agreements. Other examples include Flora, who made flowers grow; Robigus, who generated mildew; and Terminus, who guarded boundaries between plots of land. Some numina were seen as nonhuman, somewhat magical spirts that had always existed, while others were thought to be the bodiless souls of people's ancestors.

How Faunus Became a God

Unlike the famous Greek gods, whose stories continue to entertain people today, the early Roman numina lacked not only bodies but also distinct personalities, family relationships, and personal adventures. In a sense, therefore, those Roman spirits were little more than names and concepts. That explains why as a rule people did not compile and retell myths about these spirits, as the Greeks did with their own gods. The existence of this traditional vision of simplistic spiritual forces, with its lack of an accompanying mythology,

How Fortuna Chose Rome

Of the several invisible deities the early Romans worshipped, one of the most popular and important was Fortuna, goddess of chance or good luck. It remains unclear exactly when the Romans first recognized her; several modern scholars think it was sometime in the 500s or 400s BCE and that she was based on the Greek goddess of luck and fate, Tyche.

The first-century-CE Greek biographer Plutarch, who became a proud Roman citizen, wrote a short work about her (one of the dozens of essays in his large-scale work the *Moralia*). He not only praised her for helping Rome rise to greatness but also cited a brief myth about her. In that story, while searching for a country to serve, she surveyed numerous lands and peoples before recognizing the superiority of the Romans. After "she had deserted the Persians and Assyrians," Plutarch wrote, and "flitted lightly over Macedonia . . . [and] made her way through Egypt and Syria [and Carthage], . . . she took off her wings, stepped out of her sandals, and [entered] Rome . . . [where she is] present today."

Plutarch, "On the Fortune of the Romans," trans. F.C. Babbitt, Bill Thayer's website, July 14, 2018. https://penelope.uchicago.edu.

explains why the Romans based most of their myths on human leaders and heroes of the past.

Still, there were a few exceptions among the original Roman deities. In addition to Janus's tale in which he stopped an invasion of Rome, for instance, the early Roman god Faunus appeared in one myth. An overseer of fields and woodlands, he supposedly started out as a human king. Long before Rome's rise from obscurity, he ruled the Latins, an early tribal people inhabiting west-central Italy. In his story, he was such an effective and popular leader that following his death local priests prayed that he would be deified, or transformed into a god. The belief was that either the existing deities or some other mysterious heavenly force granted that request.

After becoming an immortal spirit, Faunus established an oracle—a shrine where he answered questions posed by religious pilgrims. And when the Trojan hero Aeneas reached western Italy and met a local king named Latinus, the latter consulted that oracle. Purportedly, Faunus told Latinus that he should marry his daughter to that hero from Troy.

In Awe of the Greek Gods

Although most of the numina did not have myths and colorful personalities like Janus and Faunus did, out of a respect for ancient traditions Rome's residents were long content with worshipping those invisible beings. Over time, however, this situation changed significantly. In large part this was because the Romans were avid and chronic cultural borrowers. The first-century-BCE Roman historian Sallust readily admitted this. Describing the Romans of prior generations, he wrote, "Whenever they found it suitable among allies or foes, they put in practice at home with the greatest enthusiasm, preferring to imitate rather than envy the successful."[7] Indeed, the industrious Romans copied and then improved on numerous foreign customs and devices. A well-known example is the architectural arch, borrowed from an early Italian people, the Etruscans. Over time, Etruscan-style arches became an iconic feature of Roman architecture.

None of Rome's cultural borrowings were as sweeping and far reaching, however, as those in the spiritual sphere. Through trade, conquest, and other means, Rome increasingly came into contact with Greek civilization in the last few centuries BCE. The culturally conservative Romans found themselves in awe of Greek arts and religious ideas.

In particular, the Romans found the Greek gods irresistible and compelling. In stark contrast to the numina, the Greek deities had perfect physical bodies (regularly captured by sculptors and painters), humanlike personalities, enormous powers, and reams of background stories and adventures. Seeing these beings as far more sophisticated than their traditional deities, the Romans eagerly absorbed them.

However, the numina were not abandoned and replaced. Rather, Roman religion came to associate many of the old nature spirits with Greek gods who had similar duties and characteristics. In earlier Roman society, for example, Jupiter had been a rudimentary sky spirit. In charge of thunder, he had modest powers at best. But in Rome's overhauled

The Roman god Jupiter was equated with the hugely powerful and colorful Greek deity, Zeus, depicted here.

Ceres

divine pantheon, or group of gods, that deity was equated with the hugely powerful and colorful chief Greek deity, Zeus. Likewise, Faunus became associated with the Greek woodland deity Pan; the humble Roman farming spirit Mars became the equivalent of the much stronger Greek war god Ares; the minor early Roman deity Neptune, who oversaw springs and rivers, was seen to be the same as the Greek lord of the vast seas, Poseidon; and Ceres, the Roman spirit who helped make plants grow, was equated with Demeter, Greek goddess of agriculture. A few of the old numina—Janus being one—were seen as having no Greek counterparts and hence remained the same as they were before.

Ceres's Best-Known Tale

It is important to point out that it was not just the Greek gods' physical forms and personalities that the Romans borrowed. Rome's religion also absorbed the Greek deities' myths, in most cases practically word for word. In this way large numbers of the native numina gained ready-made background stories. Ceres, for example, acquired the myths of Demeter. These captivating myths explored her family connections, deeds, and adventures. For the newly refurbished Ceres, the most crucial of those tales involved her brother Jupiter (the Greek Zeus); her daughter Proserpina (the Greek Persephone); and another brother, Pluto (the Greek Hades), ruler of the gloomy underworld.

As this well-known tale begins, Proserpina is picking flowers in a sunlit meadow, when suddenly the ground cracks open and Pluto emerges, standing on his golden chariot. Grabbing the young woman, he plunges back into the gaping earth and takes her to his dimly lit castle in the underworld. Proserpina's mother, Ceres, hears the girl's cries but is too far away to help.

Not long afterward, Ceres finds out that Pluto has abducted her daughter. In a state of extreme anger and frustration, the goddess brings forth massive droughts that destroy many food crops and cause large numbers of people to go hungry. Her brother Jupiter tries to calm her but to no avail.

The situation for humanity eventually becomes so desperate that both Jupiter and Pluto decide they must find a way to appease the distraught Ceres. To this end, the two gods approach their sister and offer her a deal. It is that Proserpina will be allowed to live with her mother on earth's surface during the spring and summer. In the fall and winter, however, the girl will dwell with her new husband in his subterranean kingdom. Ceres grudgingly accepts those terms, and in the months that followed crops begin to grow again.

The goddess Ceres (left) and her daughter Proserpina (right) reunite at the start of spring. Ceres and Pluto agreed that every year, during fall and winter, Proserpina would live with Pluto. The deal meant that during spring and summer she would live back with her mother on the surface, and crops would flourish.

A Uniquely Roman Mythology

The Romans were well aware that this and other myths borrowed from the Greeks were just that—of Greek origin. Indeed, when Ovid compiled his huge collection of such myths—the *Metamorphoses*—he simply retold the Greek versions, replacing the gods' Greek names with the Roman equivalents. This was perfectly acceptable to his readers, in large part because they did not see those stories as the mainstay of their own national mythology.

The primary thrust of that corpus of purely Roman tales consisted instead of the events and heroes of Rome's earlier centuries. Today historians know that large portions of those stories were partially or fully fictional. But in the Romans' eyes they were very real components of a venerable history in which they took enormous pride. Ovid, Livy, Virgil, and other Augustan writers supplied the Roman public with comprehensive, elegant renditions of those stories. Overall, in Jane F. Gardner's words, they

Ovid Retells the Greek Myths

One of the key factors that helped cement the popularity of the Greek myths among the Romans was the publication of Ovid's masterful book the *Metamorphoses*. Composed largely between 3 and 8 CE, it contains detailed tellings of more than 250 myths, most of them Greek, with a few native Roman ones included in the mix. This truly great literary work survived the collapse of the ancient world and experienced a new round of popularity in late medieval and early modern times. University of Newcastle scholar Marguerite Johnson calls Ovid's masterpiece

> a rollercoaster of a read. Beginning with the creation of the world, and ending with Rome in his own lifetime, the *Metamorphoses* drags the reader through time and space, from beginnings to endings, from life to death, from moments of delicious joy to episodes of depravity and abjection. Such is life, Ovid would say. . . . [The myths told in the book are] woven together by the theme of metamorphosis or transformation. The artistic dexterity involved in pulling off this literary feat is testimony to Ovid's skill and ambition as a poet.

Marguerite Johnson, "Guide to the Classics: Ovid's *Metamorphoses* and Reading Rape," The Conversation, September 13, 2016. https://theconversation.com.

"depicted Rome itself and its people as marked out by the gods to be the destined rulers of the whole world."[8]

The words "marked out by the gods" are important here, as those deities were by no means excluded from that compilation of heroic myths. In fact, Livy and other writers regularly gave the divine beings roles to play in those tales. Two well-known examples are Jupiter and his wife, Juno (the Greek Hera), in the story of Aeneas's epic journey to Italy. For reasons of her own, Juno repeatedly interferes with that hero's mission, including igniting a fire intended to burn his ships. In contrast, Jupiter, who wants Aeneas to succeed, aids him when necessary. To douse the flames of Juno's fire, for instance, the chief god sends a rainstorm.

Of particular note is that the sub-myth about Juno, Jupiter, and the fire in Aeneas's story did not exist before the Augustan age. Virgil invented it to heighten the drama of the *Aeneid*. At no other time in history did a handful of writers boldly create a new set of national myths in so short a time as Virgil, Livy, and their colleagues did. After Roman religion had been overshadowed for so long by the Greek gods and their highly entertaining myths, these writers firmly established a uniquely Roman mythology. With its tales of Roman founders, leaders, and heroes of old, all guided by divine hands, it has thrilled and inspired generation after generation of writers and readers right up to the present day.

CHAPTER TWO

Aeneas's Quest for a New Homeland

In the years of his boyhood and early manhood, Aeneas had never heard of Rome. After all, in his lifetime that now famous Italian city did not yet exist. Instead, his focus was on the independent trading city of Troy (situated in what is now northwestern Turkey), where he was one of the local princes and a leading warrior. He had attained that lofty position because his father, Anchises, was a first cousin of Troy's king, Priam. Aeneas also commanded respect because his mother was the Greek goddess of love, Aphrodite, who had had a brief affair with Anchises.

During the ten-year siege of Troy by a Greek army, Aeneas proved his bravery by slaying several enemy fighters. Yet he also came close to death himself twice. In the first episode, he engaged in single combat with the renowned Greek warrior Diomedes and survived only because Aphrodite intervened on her son's behalf. Later, Aeneas faced off with the greatest of the Greek champions—Achilles. And this time the Greek sea god Poseidon stepped in and rescued the young Trojan prince.

Poseidon's motivation for that act was that he had heard a rumor among his fellow gods that Aeneas had a crucial, world-altering destiny awaiting him after the war's conclusion. So it was important that the young man survive the conflict. Later, when the Greek soldiers entered Troy and began sacking it, writes modern mythologist Michael Stapleton, Aeneas "awoke to find the city in flames. [He] hurried to his . . . father Anchises [who was] still alive. He hoisted his father on his shoulder and took his own son, Ascanius, by the hand. [They] and a [small] band of Trojans who had managed to escape from the city, [boarded some] ships and sailed [away]."[9]

In the massive confusion surrounding the city's demise, the triumphant Greeks did not notice the departing vessels. So the small band of Trojans made good their escape. Little did Aeneas realize at that moment what fate and the gods had ordained for him. It was to sail far to the west and there establish a new, noble people who would, in the fullness of time, come to rule the known world.

Preoccupied with Beginnings

This tale of Aeneas's family background and escape from the burning Troy constitutes the start of the famous and fulsome collection of myths that tell how he founded the Roman race. The Romans came to call the totality of his great journey the *Aeneid*, after the title Virgil gave his epic poem about that grand expedition. During the roughly five centuries of Rome's existence following that work's creation, every generation of Romans looked on it as their national epic. And Aeneas stood out as one of Rome's greatest past heroes.

The Roman people were fascinated by and took enormous pride in the myths about those heroes, including Aeneas. In part this was because such stories explained why Rome had risen to greatness. Also, such tales seemed to justify its conquest of the many lands bordering the Mediterranean Sea.

Still another reason for the enduring popularity of Aeneas's myths was that they explored a key facet of Rome's beginnings. The Romans had a major preoccupation with tales about how various aspects of their civilization were established in the dim

The Greek hero Aeneas rescues his father, Anchises, and his son, Ascanius, from the burning city of Troy. The story of Aeneas and how he established the lineage that would lead the Roman people is told by the Roman poet, Vrigil.

past. Among their favorite foundation stories were those that told how the Roman people, or race, came to be; how the city of Rome itself arose; the exploits and eventual eradication of Rome's early kings; and so forth. Jane F. Gardner points out that during the reign of their first emperor, Augustus (30 BCE–14 CE), the Romans were enthralled by etiology, the study of beginnings, including "the beginning of rituals, of place-names, of institutions, of cities, of the whole Roman people and its history."[10]

A primary reason that the Romans of that period, the so-called early Empire, so tightly embraced these many foundation myths was that it met a vital need. Namely, such tales helped shape their identity as a people. To that end, Gardner says, "they used a variety of materials, such as ideas and motifs [themes] from Greek mythology and . . . stories from the family traditions of some of the great Roman families."[11]

Indeed, throughout the *Aeneid*, Virgil skillfully molds that national identity. In particular, he emphasizes that Rome is distinct among the world's nations because it was divinely chosen to rule them all. As the late historian R.H. Barrow put it, Virgil suggests that

the most significant movement of history . . . is the march of the Roman along the road of his destiny to a high civilization. For in that destiny is to be found the valid and permanent interpretation of all [human] movement and all development. . . . The stately *Aeneid* progresses throughout its length to this theme, the universal and ultimate triumph of the Roman spirit as the highest manifestation of man's powers.[12]

The Prophecy and the Flying Fiends

Aeneas's myths show that the noble Roman spirit, with its ability to command others, was present in its formative stages in his own personal character. He demonstrated his sense of decency

Aeneas's Adventures Set to Music

Virgil's *Aeneid*, which tells Aeneas's collected myths in remarkable detail, survived Rome's fall in the late 400s and early 500s CE. That pinnacle of Roman literature went on during medieval and modern times to inspire numerous artistic works, including paintings, sculptures, and musical compositions. Of the musical pieces based on Aeneas's story, one of the first was a 1689 tragic opera—*Dido and Aeneas* by English composer Henry Purcell. It deals primarily with the bittersweet, doomed love affair between Aeneas and Carthage's Queen Dido. Realizing that the man she loves will likely not return to her from Italy, she sings an aria (an operatic song) in which she says he should forget all about her. Then she kills herself. Purcell's work deals with the romance from Dido's point of view, while in comparison, the focus of the more recent opera *Aeneas and Dido* (2007) by Canadian composer James Rolfe is more from Aeneas's viewpoint. The largest-scale and most famous musical excursion into elements of Aeneas's story is French composer Hector Berlioz's opera *Les Troyens*, or *The Trojans*, composed in 1858. Some of the many major US productions of it appeared in New York in 1983, Los Angeles in 1991, and San Francisco in 2015.

and honor, for example, while the Greeks were sacking Troy. He could easily have slipped away alone, unnoticed, to save himself, but instead he also saved his father, his son, and as many other people as he could during his escape.

Also, in the days that followed, Aeneas showed his innate leadership abilities by reaching out to divine authority on behalf of his whole party. Sailing southwestward from Troy, he ordered his ships to stop briefly at the small Aegean island of Delos. There, he sought advice from the local oracle of the Greek god of prophecy, Apollo. Almost immediately, an answer came from that deity. The Trojan refugees should sail westward, Apollo said, and find the land from which their distant ancestors had originally come. Moreover, the god added, "there is a place the Greeks have called Hesperia, the western land, an ancient country powerful in war and rich of soil. The people who dwell there call themselves Italians [and] there lies your true home."[13]

Now realizing that his destiny, and that of his followers, was to resettle in faraway Italy, Aeneas gave the order to depart the Aegean Sea and head in the direction of the sunsets. Not long after entering the Mediterranean waters, the vessels' lookouts saw in the distance an island that appeared to be uncharted. Aeneas decided that it would be prudent to land there and gather badly needed supplies. So the ships dropped anchor near the beaches.

Going ashore, Aeneas and the other members of the landing party found a herd of cows and proceeded to slaughter and cook them in preparation for taking the meat to the ships. But no sooner had the aroma of the roasted beef wafted into the air than seemingly out of nowhere a swarm of hideous, foul-smelling, birdlike beasts appeared. These, Virgil explained, were the Harpies, the very same monsters earlier encountered by the Greek heroes Jason and the Argonauts. The fiendish flying females were known for ruining people's food by covering it with a disgusting stench. "They stank revoltingly," Aeneas later recalled, "and screeched appallingly."[14]

Aeneas and his men battle the hideous creatures known as Harpies.

As the creatures swooped down and began ruining the meat with their awful odors, Aeneas ordered his men to draw their swords and fight back. "My comrades charged and engaged in a new form of battle," he remembered, "trying to wound those disgusting birds of the sea."[15] These efforts proved futile, however, as the Harpies managed to elude the swishing sword blades. Having made most of the cooked beef inedible, all but one of the creatures flew away. That lone winged gargoyle now spoke to the Trojans. First it claimed the cattle had belonged to the Harpies, and then it delivered a prophecy. Aeneas and the others would reach Italy, but they would become so hungry they would end up eating their own tables.

Italy and a Prophecy Fulfilled

Aeneas had no idea what this cryptic prediction might mean. He focused instead on the talking Harpy's assurance that the refugees would indeed reach Italy. And he took hope from that thought. Several months later the ships reached the island of Sicily, lying just off the coast of southern Italy. There, Aeneas's father died. The Trojans were in the midst of holding his funeral rites when a huge storm struck, and its howling winds forced the vessels out to sea and southward, away from Italy.

The onslaught of this tempest was no coincidence. Juno, mighty Jupiter's divine wife, had conjured up the storm in an effort to prevent the ships from reaching Italy. She knew that if the Roman race did spring from Aeneas and Rome did rise to greatness, it would destroy Carthage in the three conflicts known as the Punic Wars. Situated on Africa's northern shore, Carthage was, as Virgil put it, the "city Juno favored of all the world the most, [and] she yearned to see [it someday] ruling the world."[16]

Virgil and Augustus

The people of Rome called the author of the epic *Aeneid* Virgil for short, and that appellation for him remained throughout the centuries right up to the present. His full name, however, was Publius Vergilius Maro. Born in 70 BCE, he grew up in northern Italy and as a young man journeyed to Rome in hopes of becoming a published writer. Because of his intelligence and formidable talent, he was soon welcomed into a circle of popular poets and in time became arguably the greatest among them. Through his various connections among these and other upper-class Romans, Virgil eventually met and became friends with the young Octavian, Julius Caesar's adopted son. Later, Octavian became Rome's first emperor, Augustus, and it was to him that Virgil dedicated his masterwork, the *Aeneid*. In fact, the poet was careful to mention his high-placed friend in the work. When Aeneas visits his father in the underworld and the old man shows him Rome's future history, Virgil's words suggest that all of that history was destined to lead to Rome's greatest ruler of all—none other than Augustus.

By a twist of fate, it was Carthage where the ships, tossed wildly around by the gale, eventually landed. There, Aeneas fell in love with the city's queen, Dido, who loved him back with extraordinary intensity. Yet the young man's sense of duty and destiny led him to leave her behind and once more strive to reach Italy's shores.

Juno continued to try to prevent Aeneas from fulfilling his destiny. But her husband, Jupiter, who strongly supported the prophesied rise of Rome, made sure her efforts ultimately failed. Only a few weeks after leaving Carthage, Aeneas finally landed in southwestern Italy. There, a local sorceress—the Sibyl—told him he should sail further northward to the Tiber River and plain of Latium.

Not long after Aeneas's ships entered the Tiber, he ordered a rest stop and lunch break. After he and his followers had finished the meal, they still felt hungry, so they decided to eat the thin bread cakes they were using as platters. In a sudden burst of comprehension, Aeneas interpreted these to be their "tables," which meant that the Harpy's seemingly meaningless prophecy had, in an unexpected way, been fulfilled.

Birth of the Noblest People

In the months that followed, the Trojans got to know the locals, who belonged to a tribal group known as Latins. Also, Aeneas became friends with the region's king, Latinus, and his daughter, Lavinia. It did not take long for Aeneas to ask for the young woman's hand in marriage, and he was disappointed to hear that Turnus, a member of a neighboring people, the Rutulians, had already proposed to her.

Aeneas (shown holding his sword) battles Turnus for the hand of the woman he hoped to marry, Lavinia.

In this way, Aeneas and Turnus became adversaries. It quickly became clear to everyone that their rivalry was bound to lead to bloodshed. And in time the two men did in fact meet in single combat, "struggling for footing, swords flashing," the late modern myth teller Norma L. Goodrich wrote. "Blow after blow they landed until the blood flowed from a hundred cuts." As Turnus tried to wipe off the blood clouding his vision, "Aeneas raised [his] spear and hurled it."[17] Seconds later, Turnus's body lay unmoving in the dirt.

Aeneas and Lavinia were now free to marry, and after the ceremony they established a new town, called Lavinium in her honor. In fulfillment of divine prophecy, their long and contented union marked the merger of the Trojan and Latin races. A new family line had been created, one that held the spark of a new and noble race—the Romans. As Jupiter had earlier predicted, they were fated to march in humanity's forefront. Regarding the Romans, he said, "I see no measure nor date, and I grant them dominion [supreme power] without end. . . . Yes, even Juno will mend her ways and vie with me in cherishing the Romans, the master race, the wearers of the toga. So it is willed!"[18]

With these words, the chief god foretold Rome's rise to enormous military and political power. No less important were his words "without end." They suggested that that power would last for all eternity.

Romulus Founds Rome, the Eternal City

Thanks to Aeneas and his followers, Livy wrote in the late first century BCE, "it was already written in the book of fate that this great city of ours [Rome] should arise, and the first steps taken to the founding of the mightiest empire the world has known."[19] The next major step after Aeneas's contributions to this process, Livy went on, was the appearance of the city's actual founder, Romulus. The latter belonged to the thirteenth generation in the family line established by Aeneas.

Key to Romulus's birth and rise to power was what happened in the generation preceding his own. At that time his grandfather, Numitor, was king of Alba Longa, a colony of Lavinium, the city Aeneas had founded. One day Numitor's power-hungry brother, Amulius, usurped the throne and slew the former ruler's sons, so that none of Numitor's descendants could lay claim to the kingship.

This situation changed, however, when Numitor's daughter, Rhea Silvia, was raped. She soon gave birth to twin boys, Romulus and Remus, thereby producing two possible new heirs to Numitor's throne. The furious Amulius had Rhea Silvia cruelly chained in a dungeon and told one of his henchmen to go drown the babies in the Tiber.

Fortunately for the infants, the man tasked with killing them did not toss them straight into the water. Instead, he placed them in a basket and set that carrier adrift in the river. After he departed, some gusts of wind pushed the water near the shore back a bit, leaving the basket on a small patch of dry soil. At that point, in Livy's words, a she-wolf "heard the children crying and made her way to where they were. She offered them her teats to suck and treated them with such gentleness that [a shepherd named] Faustulus . . . found her licking them with her tongue. Faustulus took them to his hut and gave them to his wife Larentia to nurse."[20]

Thanks to the kindly couple, the boys grew into healthy, stalwart young men. Faustulus had correctly guessed that they were the royal twins rumored to have died in the river years before. He decided he must reveal to them their true heritage. Thereafter, Romulus and his brother helped Numitor slay Amulius and regain the throne. The two brothers, Livy wrote, "saluted their grandfather as king, and by a shout of unanimous consent [from the citizenry] his royal title was confirmed."[21]

A Past to Be Proud Of

This tale of twin boys who were saved by a wolf and raised by shepherds is one of the numerous separate myths making up the epic story of the founding of the city of Rome by Romulus. In Rome's folklore about its major past heroes, Romulus was second only to Aeneas. As was true of the latter's saga of launching the Roman race, the story of Romulus's creation of Rome itself served two crucial purposes in Roman eyes. First, Romulus's achievements told the Romans where they came from and gave them a concrete past. To them, it appeared to be an actual history, and one that they could be proud of. As Jane F. Gardner puts it, those tales of Rome's earliest days "enabled the Romans to claim their own place in the tradition that was regarded as in a sense 'historical.'"[22]

Second, the myths of Rome's supposedly brave and noble early founders improved the image Rome projected to foreigners across the Mediterranean world. Implicit in that image was that Rome was not just another of the many unremarkable tribes and kingdoms that came and went in early Italy. Rather, its ancient, venerable past made it appear more legitimate and worthy. The tales of Rome's founding gave its people "a respectable identity in the eyes of a wider world," noted scholar T.J. Cornell points out. And that impressive identity "could be used to advantage in [Rome's] dealings with the Greeks [and other non-Romans]."[23]

Indeed, the leaders of the Roman Republic and Roman Empire could brag to foreign rulers and diplomats that their upright

The twin babies, Romulus and Remus, were found by a shepherd named Faustulus, who gave them to his wife, Larentia, to nurse.

Modern historians grant that most of the surviving myths about Rome's earliest few centuries contain plenty of exaggeration, distortion, and fabricated episodes. Yet thanks to the results of archaeological discoveries made in the past century, the experts also suspect that some elements in those tales are at least based on real happenings. It appears certain, for example, that the Sabines played a crucial role in Rome's early growth. First, several of the original patrician (noble and wealthy) families inhabiting the city in those days seem to have come from Sabine stock. The best-known example was Attus Clausus, from the Sabine town of Regillus. After moving to the infant Rome, he established the noble Claudian family line that over time produced several senators and eventually the emperors Tiberius (reigned 14–37 CE) and Claudius (41–54 CE). Numerous other Sabines moved to early Rome. At the same time, most of the nearby Sabine towns opened trade relations with Rome, thereby aiding in the city's early economic growth. Owing to the fact that Sabine culture contributed so much to early Rome, it is not surprising that the Sabines feature so prominently in several older Roman myths.

founder, Romulus, was no mere common farmer or laborer. Rather, he came from a long-standing royal family line. And that alone gave Rome a certain degree of credibility.

The Perfect Place for a City

Still, Romulus's main claim to fame was not his royal blood but instead his notable collection of personal qualities. These included his lofty ambitions, earnestness, cleverness, willingness to work hard, determination, and most of all, superior leadership qualities. According to Livy, Plutarch, and other Greco-Roman historians, Romulus demonstrated all of these impressive traits in the years following his and his brother's success in reinstalling their grandfather on Alba Longa's throne.

With that impressive feat behind them, the twins decided to establish a new city of their own. They started by investigating the wilderness areas lying near the fertile Latium plain and eventually found a spot they felt was perfect. It consisted of seven low hills not far from a bend in the Tiber and the lands surrounding them.

Both young men were eager to get started with the new project. As it turned out, however, Remus did not live long enough to see the town's first buildings rise. He and Romulus had a bitter falling-out that ended in tragedy. According to Livy, the two got into a nasty argument over which of them would govern the new city. Alternate myths about the quarrel have survived, one of which claims the brothers searched for mystical bird signs sent by the gods. Remus, Livy said, saw six eagles flying in formation, whereas, "double the number of birds appeared [for] Romulus." Supposedly, that meant the gods favored Romulus above Remus, and the latter died when the two men resorted to swordplay over the issue. In the other story, Livy wrote, Remus made fun of his brother, after which "Romulus killed him in a fit of rage."[24]

Whichever version was closer to the truth, Remus lost his life, leaving his twin as Rome's solitary founder. Romulus now showed his realistic, practical side by admitting he could not erect an entire town with his own hands. Wisely, he sent for carpenters, masons, and laborers from the Etruscan towns situated not far north of the seven hills. They aided him in laying out streets and installing foundations for houses, temples, and other structures. In addition, defensive walls had to be created in order to keep would-be attackers at bay. None of the cities in the general region seemed threatening at the time, the founder realized. But there was no guarantee that peace would always prevail. Sooner or later, he reasoned, such defenses would be needed.

Laws, Lictors, and New Citizens

While the buildings and protective walls were slowly but steadily rising, Romulus also devoted attention to matters of organization and government. All the cities and kingdoms he knew of had local laws and legal institutions. Without them, he instinctually realized, disorder would reign, and as Livy put it, "a unified people and government would not have been possible." Hence, in another wise move, Romulus "summoned his subjects and gave them laws." There also should be symbols of the government's authority, Romulus rea-

Romulus directs the building of the wall that he believed would one day be needed to keep anyone attacking Rome at bay.

soned. As Livy wrote, the citizens "could be induced to respect the law only if he himself adopted certain visible signs of power. He proceeded, therefore, to increase the dignity and impressiveness of the throne and government."[25] One of these signs of power Romulus introduced consisted of twelve men called lictors; their job was to walk with the king wherever he went in public and to carry axes symbolizing the king's power to execute people who broke the laws.

Meanwhile, as Romulus dealt with these logistical issues, Livy continued, "Rome was growing. More and more ground was coming within the circuit of its walls." In those days, according to Livy, someone who created a new city and wanted to increase the population routinely rounded up

a lot of homeless and destitute folk . . . [and] Romulus now followed a similar course. To help fill up his big new town, he [made it] a place of asylum for fugitives. Here fled for refuge all the [outcasts] from the neighboring peoples, some free, some slaves, and all of them wanting nothing more than a fresh start. That mob was the first real addition to the city's strength, the first step toward her future greatness.[26]

Plutarch: Biographer, Moralist, and Myth Teller

In addition to his detailed overview of Romulus's life and achievements, the noted Greek writer Plutarch penned numerous other biographies of Roman statesmen and military generals. He was born in about 46 CE in a small city situated north of Athens, Greece, and as a young man became involved in government affairs in his home town. A gifted writer, he soon began devoting most of his time to producing essays of varied lengths on a wide array of subjects. These efforts did not go unnoticed in Greek and Roman educated circles, and he gained many high-placed Roman friends. In turn, he became a Roman citizen and for a while lived and worked in Rome. In the years that followed, Plutarch turned out his most famous work—the *Parallel Lives*—a large-scale collection of fifty highly detailed biographies of well-known Roman and Greek rulers, city founders, military leaders, and various controversial figures. He also wrote another hefty work—the *Moralia*, or *Moral Essays*. An assortment of short, pithy articles, it includes discussions of political, philosophic, scientific, ethical, and other issues of his day. Both the biographies and essays feature frequent overviews of and references to Roman myths, some major and others minor.

Romulus's Bold Plan

Although Romulus was happy to see so many outsiders flocking to his new settlement, he early on recognized a serious problem that needed to be addressed. Namely, the vast majority of these early settlers were men. A consistently perceptive and realistic individual, he calculated that the new city would not continue to grow unless most of those male citizens could find brides and establish new families.

One of the Roman founder's most famous myths tells how he conceived a bold plan that he was confident would rectify the city's dearth of females. First, he sent messengers to several neighboring towns. Those couriers carried formal invitations to a large religious festival to be held in Rome's main square. In addition to sacrifices to the gods, the invitations stated, there would be some entertaining athletic games and theatrical performances of various kinds. The inhabitants of these towns, most of them situated to the northeast of Rome, were members of an early Latin tribe known as the Sabines.

Close to two thousand Sabines—male and female alike—showed up in Rome for the advertised festivities. They had no idea about Romulus's plan, the details of which he had shared with hundreds of Roman men. At the height of the celebration, at the founder's signal, the plot went into effect. Each of the briefed Roman men suddenly grabbed hold of the nearest young Sabine woman and ran off with her to his house. Shocked, the girls' relatives fled to their various settlements and spread the word about the incident.

The next day Romulus sent messengers to those towns, who told the residents that the few hundred young maidens were unharmed and in no danger. In fact, they were to be well treated—almost revered—as wives of selected Roman men. Not surprisingly, the Sabines rejected these words and in the days that followed organized war parties of soldiers with orders to march on Rome and retrieve their kidnapped women.

A Major Key to Rome's Success

After some preliminary skirmishes outside the city, a large force of armed Sabines entered Rome. Two different mythological traditions have survived for what happened next. In one, the Roman god Janus unleashed a torrent of scalding-hot water on the intruders, driving them away.

Accepted by far more ancient writers, however, among them Livy and Plutarch, was the second tradition, which went as follows. First, a large battle took place on the small, flat plain situated between the Palatine and Capitoline Hills. A number of soldiers from both sides died there. But the Sabines eventually prevailed and seized a Roman fortification atop a nearby hill. Not long afterward, Romulus regrouped his men, who marched out to engage the invaders in a second battle. The Sabines, meanwhile, started to descend the hill, expecting to lose many of their own number even if they won.

But to the utter surprise of all, an event totally unforeseen occurred. Shortly before the two masses of fighters would have crashed together, the young women who had earlier been kidnapped ran out and stood between the two armies. With raised voices, the women produced "miserable cries," in Plutarch's words. "Like creatures possessed, [they approached] their husbands and their fathers [and called] now upon the Sabines, now upon the Romans, in the most tender and endearing words."[27] The overall message of those words was that the women refused to watch their fathers, brothers, and new husbands brutally slay one another. The two sides *must* negotiate a treaty, the women declared.

So moved were Romulus and the Sabine general, Titus Tatius, that they met and hammered out the very agreement the women had called for. Thereafter, the Romans and Sabines patched up their differences, and most of the residents of the Sabine towns moved to Rome and became citizens. Moreover, for a few years Romulus and Tatius ruled Rome jointly.

Modern historians suggest that this mythical treaty with the Sabines may have been based on a real early agreement be-

In order to avoid bloodshed, Sabine women stood between the Roman and Sabine soldiers and insisted that a peace treaty be negotiated.

tween the two peoples. Over the centuries a major key to the Romans' success was actually their gift for political negotiation. Rather than treat former enemies cruelly, they made treaties with them and granted them Roman citizenship, further expanding the realm. The Romans had "a talent for patient political reasonableness that was unique in the ancient world," the late historian Michael Grant said. "On the whole, Rome [displayed] a self-restraint, a readiness to compromise, and a calculated generosity that the world had never seen."[28] Furthermore, the myths associated with Romulus suggest that in his wisdom, he introduced that prudent policy, which would serve untold millions of future Romans exceedingly well.

CHAPTER FOUR

Heroes Who Sacrificed All for Rome

During the initial years of the Roman Empire, Rome's main square, the Forum, featured a small, shallow pond that people called the Lacus Curtius, or Curtius's Pool. The great historian Livy reported that there were multiple mythical traditions for how that pool formed. The one most likely to be true, he wrote, was the tale of a brave early Roman hero named Marcus Curtius.

More than three centuries before his own time, Livy said, an awful plague ravaged the city. Even worse, it came during a time of political strife in Rome, and many people thought things could not get much worse. In this, they were wrong. For one day, without warning, a large chasm appeared in the midst of the Forum. When some nearby witnesses summoned the nerve to approach the hole and inspect it, Livy recalled, they could not see the bottom.

The city's leaders, a group that included local priests, met in hopes of determining the cause of the chasm's formation and what to do about it. They concluded that the pit must have been created by an angry god. Clearly, the chief priests argued, the only way to get rid of the pit was to offer a valuable sacrifice that would appease whichever deity the Romans had displeased.

While further discussions of the matter were in progress, Marcus Curtius, a young soldier of some distinction, heard about the impending sacrifice. He feared that the city's leaders were not acting fast enough. He felt sure that the ceremony must take place immediately in order to prevent the chasm from expanding and swallowing the entire city. To that end, he volunteered to sacrifice himself for the good of his country.

The authorities accepted this courageous offer and made sure he was dressed in the finest garments and strongest armor available. Then, as Livy told it, Curtius mounted a horse. He rode to the edge of the pit, "and stretching out his hands first to the heavens and then to the yawning gulf in the ground . . . he devoted himself to death."[29]

Seconds later, Livy continued, the young man plunged "into the chasm, [after which] a crowd of men and women threw piles of offerings and fruits of the earth in after him."[30] Mere minutes later, the story goes, the ground shook violently and the chasm rapidly closed, leaving behind a shallow depression that subsequently filled with rainwater. It became known as Curtius's Pool, Livy said, in honor of that brave youth who willingly gave his life that Rome might survive.

A Blend of Historical and Legendary Events

The story of Marcus Curtius's valiant sacrifice is but one of many examples of the most common, and to the ancient Romans most popular, theme in their collected myths. It consists of the exploits of heroes of previous generations who gave their all in one way or another for the good of Rome and its people. Some of those distinguished individuals were, like Curtius, military figures. Others were upper-class men and women from noble families. Still others were simple farmers or other ordinary commoners who, under extraordinary circumstances, rose to the occasion and saved the day.

The setting of most of those heroic myths was a period encompassing Rome's Monarchy (ca. 753 to ca. 510 BCE), when kings ruled the city, and the early Republic (established ca. 509 BCE). That era seemed extremely distant to the Romans of Livy's time, close to five centuries later. No detailed written histories were compiled during that formative period of Rome. This meant that later historians like Livy and Plutarch had to rely on a mix of oral storytelling and scattered written documents passed down to them through many generations.

That mass of information from the past contained snippets of real historical information. But it was also full of exaggeration and folklore. To their credit, Livy and other later Greco-Roman writers dismissed the most outlandish claims, yet they accepted much of the rest as historical. As a result, although Romulus, Curtius, and other early heroes may (or in some cases may not) have been

Marcus Curtius prepares to sacrifice himself by plunging into the chasm that had opened in the midst of Rome's Forum.

The feats of Rome's ancient heroes—including Aeneas, Romulus, Curtius, Horatius Cocles, Scaevola, and numerous others—became potent sources of inspiration for painters, sculptors, printmakers, and other Renaissance and early modern European artists. For example, *Aeneas Fleeing the Burning Troy* became the title of dozens of paintings by European artists. One of the finest of these is a 1598 work by Italy's Federico Barocci. As for Romulus and his brother Remus, they were the subjects of a 1616 painting by the great Belgian artist Peter Paul Rubens. The engraving shows the shepherd Faustulus finding the young twins being cared for by a female wolf. Meanwhile, the legendary hero Horatius, who repelled the Etruscans at the bridge, appeared in a 1586 engraving by Dutch printmaker Hendrick Goltzius. Showing that warrior decked out in full armor, it is still used today in books and online articles that mention Horatius. Another famous European artwork is a stone sculpture that shows Gaius Mucius Scaevola purposely thrusting his hand into the flames. Carved by Frenchman Louis-Pierre Deseine in 1791, it now rests in Paris's Louvre Museum.

real people, some of their deeds are likely semi-historical at best. Much of Roman mythology is therefore a complex blend of historical and legendary events and characters.

The Romans of Livy's time and the four centuries that followed tended to see the old heroic myths as largely true, in part because they provided the nation with a viable history. Also, the supposed deeds of those heroes of the past provided much inspiration for brave and righteous conduct on the part of Romans in each new generation. During the late Republic and into the Empire, Jane F. Gardner points out, "the noblest Roman families were particularly proud to include such stories in their family histories, and . . . continued for a long time to model their conduct upon them." They felt that the deeds of those bygone heroes "exemplified the virtues that the Romans liked to think were part of the essential Roman character."[31]

Brave Horatius at the Bridge

Certainly every male Roman, no matter his age, at one time or another dreamed of being as fearless as one of Rome's most heroic early figures—Horatius Cocles. His timeless tale harkens back to a time when Rome was young and threatened by an Etruscan army. Those soldiers were led by their king, Lars Porsenna, who was bent on conquering the still small Roman city-state.

When word spread that the enemy force was on the march, thousands of Roman farmers fled their fields and hurried to take refuge in the urban center, a cluster of government buildings, temples, and houses situated on the town's seven hills. At the time only one bridge—the Sublician—crossed over the Tiber's turbulent waters, giving access to that center. A small group of Roman warriors, Horatius Cocles among them, helped the last civilians cross the bridge. Then those soldiers started to chop down the structure's main supports. The plan was to make it collapse so the invaders could not enter the city's hub.

The men were only partway through their demolition efforts when the Etruscans appeared in the distance and headed straight for the bridge. Seeing this, Horatius told his comrades to keep chopping, ran to the front of the bridge, and prepared to meet the oncoming army on his own. A few minutes later, Livy wrote, the Etruscans "paused in sheer astonishment at such reckless courage." How, they wondered, could only one man hope to repel thousands? They soon received their answer, as Horatius boldly challenged them "one after another to single combat, and mocked them." At the top of his voice, he called them slaves and accused them of caring not for "their own liberty," since they "were coming to destroy the liberty of others."[32]

Hearing these words, the men in the Etruscan front ranks were surprised and horrified to see Horatius slay more than a dozen of the finest

fighters Lars Porsenna could muster. Then the lone Roman began killing the attackers two and three at a time. Soon the piles of bodies he created made it difficult for more soldiers to reach him.

Highly irritated by this incredible display of fortitude, Porsenna considered having his archers kill Horatius. But at that moment the ax-swinging Romans managed to destroy the bridge's last support. With a loud creaking sound, the massive structure abruptly toppled into the river, taking Horatius with it. Although injured, he survived. And because he saved the city, his thankful countrymen later honored him by erecting a statue of him in the Forum.

The Patriotic Assassin

Another legendary early hero whom the later Romans accepted as a real historical figure was Gaius Mucius Scaevola. His last name means "left-handed" in Latin, and his myth explains how he earned that nickname. The story takes place a few months after

43

Livy's Masterwork

Titus Livius, known as Livy for short, was a major historian during Rome's late Republic and early Empire. Born in 59 BCE in Patavium (modern Padua) in northern Italy, he lived most of his life in Rome. There he wrote his masterwork, *Ab urbe condita libri*, which translates into English as *History of Rome from Its Foundation*. In its original form it comprised 142 volumes (each consisting of a single papyrus scroll). Only 35 of those books have survived. The first several contain hundreds of stories about early Rome, many of them now seen as myths. They include tales about Rome's founder and first king, Romulus; the other kings who followed him; Marcus Curtius, who plunged into a giant sinkhole to save his city; Horatius Cocles, who fought an enemy army single-handedly; Cloelia and other female Roman heroes; and numerous others. Whether the people he described were authentic historical figures or mythical ones, Livy possessed extraordinary writing skills. Moreover, he was blessed, the late literary scholar J. Wight Duff said, with "the gift of enthusiasm for olden times, olden heroes, and olden virtues." And his great masterwork "is unsurpassed in its [faithfulness] to Rome's national character."

J. Wight Duff, *A Literary History of Rome, from the Origins to the Close of the Golden Age*. New York: Barnes & Noble, 1963, pp. 473–74.

Horatius managed to keep the Etruscans out of Rome's urban center. Not surprisingly, Porsenna was angry that his attack had failed, but he refused to give up on conquering Rome. Over time he brought in siege equipment, planning to surround the Romans and starve them into submission.

Seeing what the Etruscans were doing, on his own Scaevola conceived a possible way to stop them. He approached the city's leaders and, according to Livy, told them, "I wish to cross the river and [infiltrate] the enemy's lines."[33] Once in the Etruscan camp, the young man said, he would find Porsenna and stab him to death.

His daring scheme approved, Scaevola crossed the river under cover of darkness and evaded the enemy camp's guards. In the camp's center, he saw two elegantly dressed men sitting on a raised platform, which was surrounded by dozens of soldiers. Unsure which of the two men was the king, Scaevola took a guess. He suddenly jumped up onto the platform and stabbed the closer of the two men. After several guards seized the young

Roman, he discovered that the man he had killed was not Porsenna but rather his secretary.

The king himself soon questioned Scaevola and demanded to know why he had slain the secretary. According to Livy, Scaevola answered, "I am a Roman. My name is Gaius Mucius. I came here to kill you . . . [and] I have as much courage to die as to kill. It is our Roman way to do and to suffer bravely."[34]

Porsenna now threatened to have the young man burned alive if he did not reveal some of Rome's weaknesses. Seemingly unphased by those words, Scaevola smiled and walked to a nearby torch. There, he thrust his right hand into the flames and held it unmoving, without crying out, as his flesh blackened and sizzled. Astounded, Porsenna ordered his guards to pull the man's hand out of the fire. The king admitted that he had never before witnessed such raw courage and then told Scaevola he was free to leave.

The would-be assassin, Scaevola, holds his hand over a flame as Porsenna, the Etruscan leader (seated), looks on. Impressed by Scaevola's courage, Porsenna ordered the young Roman released.

Before departing, the young Roman offered the king a morsel of advice, namely, "Since you respect courage, I will tell you in gratitude what you could not force from me by threats."[35] There were over three hundred other young Roman patriots like himself, he said. And each would gladly give his life to stop the siege.

After Scaevola had departed, Porsenna seriously pondered the young man's words. Would the royal guards be able to detect and deter every one of the hundreds of Roman assassins? Reasoning that sooner or later one of them would succeed, Porsenna decided it was probably too dangerous to fight the Romans. The next day he sent a messenger to Rome to announce that he wanted to make peace.

A True Roman Hero

Meanwhile, the Roman people welcomed Scaevola as a true hero. For his bravery in facing down the enemy king and losing a hand in the process, the government gave him a prime piece of farmland on the Tiber's right bank. As for Scaevola himself, like other Roman heroes before and after him, he remained humble. He had no problem being called by his new nickname—"left-handed"— for it was like a badge of honor. In any case, he felt that a hand was but a small price to pay to ensure the survival of his country. For as every young Roman was taught, Rome had been singled out by the gods for everlasting life and glory.

CHAPTER FIVE

Brave, Patriotic Women of Rome's Past

The story of the sacrifice and death of one of Roman mythology's best-known female heroes begins in 451 BCE. At least that is the date the Romans of the late Republic and early Empire reckoned that her death took place. After the passage of some four centuries, no one could be sure. In that year, it was said, a committee of well-to-do men drew up Rome's first written laws—the famous Twelve Tables. Unfortunately for the Roman people, one of those city elders cared about neither the issue of legality nor the public good. Appius Claudius by name, he wanted to become a dictator and impose his own whims on the people. With the aid of some other rich, powerful men, he managed to seize control of the government.

Well before committing that unlawful act, the tyrant had lusted after a young maiden named Verginia, the daughter of a widely respected military general—Verginius. That virtuous young woman had several times refused Appius's advances. Now that he was the most powerful person in Rome, he tried again, this time sure she would comply. But still again she courageously rebuffed him. Furious, Appius resorted to, in Livy's words, "a method of compulsion such as only a heartless tyrant could devise."[36]

That method consisted of demanding that the young woman show up in the public court the following day. The next morning, Livy said, "the excitement in the city reached a new height. Verginius entered the Forum leading his daughter by the hand."[37] When the proceeding began, the dictator shocked everyone present by illegally making himself the chief judge. Minutes later, he claimed that by order of the court, Verginia was no longer a free Roman citizen. Instead, she was a slave who belonged to him and therefore must do his bidding.

Leaping to his feet, Verginius vigorously protested. But Appius overruled him. It looked like the tyrant would soon send soldiers to take the young woman into custody. And feeling there was no other choice, Verginia told her father that death would be preferable to slavery and rape. Also, her sacrifice might inflame the citizenry to depose the tyrant by force, saving Rome from possible ruin. Reluctantly, Verginius agreed. "He snatched a knife from a butcher . . . [and] stabbed her in the heart," Livy wrote. Then to Appius, who was standing nearby, he shouted, "May the cause of this blood rest upon your head forever!"[38]

Verginia's death did, as she and her father had hoped, subsequently move large numbers of Romans to resist the dictator. Many powerful military men and politicians joined Verginius in overthrowing the detestable Appius, who committed suicide while languishing in prison. In this way, Verginia joined the ranks of several patriotic Roman women who committed acts of valor for the good of their country and its people.

A Powerful Sense of Patriotism

Although most modern historians doubt that Verginia ever actually existed, she was very real to later generations of Romans. Whether mythical or real, her admirable attitude and deeds symbolized something fundamental in ancient Roman society. Namely, she embodied certain basic qualities that an ideal woman should possess. In her case the most obvious of those traits was a powerful sense of patriotism.

At first glance, such devotion by a Roman woman to the government and country itself might seem somewhat odd. After all, Rome had a strongly male chauvinist society in which women could neither vote nor hold public office and were expected to be completely subservient to men. Indeed, "for the most part," historian Mark Cartwright points out, "Roman women were closely identified with their perceived role in society—the duty of looking

The Roman general Verginius prepares to slay his own daughter Virginia in order to prevent her from being enslaved by the would-be dictator, Appius Claudius.

after the home and to nurture a family, in particular, to bear legitimate children. . . . The Roman family was male-dominated . . . [and] women were subordinate."[39]

Nevertheless, Roman society did recognize women's contributions as crucial in certain areas. Mythology, especially tales of the deeds of heroes of past ages, was one of those areas. All Roman men readily expressed pride in and thanks for what certain heroic women had done for Rome in the past.

Furthermore, those famous female patriots served as role models for Roman women and men. Their virtues and abilities included a sense of morality and strength of character that made Roman society stronger and more resilient. In Jane F. Gardner's words, this was reflected in various situations in which women quietly provided moral and other support behind the scenes for the male fighters and leaders. "For the Romans," she says, the stories about mythical women "had the same original purpose as the tales about Rome's male heroes. It was to encourage accep-

Pleading with Her Traitorous Son

Among the famous Roman stories that English playwright William Shakespeare dramatized was that of the traitor Coriolanus and his stalwart mother, Volumnia. The play *Coriolanus* was written sometime between 1605 and 1610. Like the myth it was based on, the play contains a climactic scene between the title character and his mother. Volumnia passionately calls on her errant son to save, rather than attack, his native land. She warns him that if he does attack, his name will be hated forever. She says in part:

> Either thou must, as a foreign recreant [traitor], be led with manacles [chains] through our streets, or else triumphantly tread on thy country's ruin . . . having bravely shed thy wife and children's blood. . . . Thou shalt no sooner march to assault thy country than to tread [upon] thy mother's womb that brought thee into this world. . . . If thou conquer Rome, the benefit which thou shalt thereby reap is such a name [for you] whose repetition will be dogged with curses. . . . [That] name [will remain] to the ensuing age abhorred [hated]. . . . Thou are not honest and the gods will plague thee.

Quoted in William Shakespeare, *Coriolanus*, Act 5, Scene 3.

tance of Roman moral priorities, in particular self-control and self-discipline, in the interests of the Roman state and its security."[40]

Tribute to a Fearless Young Woman

In the annals of early Roman myths, a young woman named Cloelia became particularly well known for displaying all those positive qualities. Seen through the eyes of Romans in later centuries, she joined the gallant ranks of Horatius and Scaevola in opposing the Etruscan conqueror Lars Porsenna. When the latter had tried to capture Rome, Horatius had mightily impressed him with his bravery by single-handedly stopping the Etruscans from crossing the bridge leading into the city. Yet that act had also greatly frustrated Porsenna, who realized that he had to devise a different approach to taking Rome.

Cloelia

A courageous Roman maiden who escaped from the Etruscans by swimming across the Tiber River

With that in mind, one of the king's advisers pointed out a possible strategy. Even before reaching the bridge, the adviser said, some of Porsenna's soldiers had seized the Janiculum Hill (which in those days was situated outside the city limits). And control of that piece of Roman land might allow the king to make certain demands of the Romans.

The first such demand Porsenna made was for Roman leaders to give him three dozen hostages. Only then would he remove his soldiers from the Janiculum. Rome's leaders felt they had no choice but to comply, because losing control of the Janiculum was simply unthinkable. The next day, therefore, the hostages made their way to the Janiculum and surrendered to the Etruscans.

Cloelia was among those prisoners. A fearless individual, no sooner was she in custody than she started formulating ways to escape. "With a number of other girls who had consented to follow her," Livy wrote, "she eluded the guards, swam across the river under a hail of missiles, and brought her company safe to Rome."[41]

Cloelia (seated on the white horse) was given to the Etruscan leader, Porsenna, as a hostage. Impressed by Cloelia's courage when she organized an escape with some other female prisoners (pictured), Porsenna freed her.

Hearing what had happened, Porsenna was angrier than ever. He threatened to keep the hill permanently if Cloelia was not returned to him. Rome's worried leaders forced her to go back to the Etruscan camp. There she came face-to-face with the king himself. He had had time to cool down and think matters through, he told her. Marveling at her courage, he said that if the situation were reversed, he would want an Etruscan woman to do exactly as she had done. To honor Cloelia's bravery, therefore, he set her free. And when she entered her beloved city the second time, an enormous crowd of well-wishers welcomed her with shouts of praise. Later, Livy added, the government gave her an "unprecedented honor: a statue representing her on horseback."[42]

The Power of a Mother's Words

About half a century after Porsenna's failure to conquer Rome, another aggressive Italian people, the Volscians, sought to capture the still small Roman city-state. And during that conflict another righteous Roman woman—Volumnia—distinguished herself. At the height of the war, her son, a Roman military officer named Gnaeus Marcius Coriolanus, was praised for skillfully capturing a Volscian town. Though a talented soldier, he was socially awkward and viewed himself as superior to most other Romans. And after he insulted one too many people, the government banished him.

Of all the places Coriolanus might have gone, he chose the Volscian capital, whose people welcomed him. Thereafter, he led a Volscian army against his own homeland, and the soldiers he commanded surrounded Rome. At that point, Volumnia came to the fore. On her own accord, she risked death by leading a small group of women to the enemy camp, where her son agreed to meet with her. She demanded to know why

The Great Mother Comes to Rome

Cybele, the goddess whom Claudia Quinta was said to personally welcome to Rome, was frequently referred to as the Great Mother across the ancient Mediterranean world. Originating in Phrygia (in west-central Anatolia), she was mainly a fertility goddess who, people believed, could also cure certain diseases and protect the residents of war-torn countries. The Greeks were familiar with her as early as the 400s BCE, and the Romans began worshipping her in 204 BCE, shortly before the end of the Second Punic War. That year some Roman ambassadors traveled to Phrygia and brought her sacred black stone (today thought to be a meteorite) back to Rome. On the return trip, Claudia's myth claims, she convinced the goddess to join the existing Roman gods. Whether or not that event actually happened, the stone was placed within a special temple the Romans erected for Cybele on Rome's Palatine Hill. About two centuries later, her annual public festival, the Megalesia, observed from April 4 to April 10, became widely popular throughout the rapidly expanding Roman Empire.

Volumnia confronts her son, Coriolanus, whose soldiers had surrounded Rome and were threatening to attack the city. Moved by his mother's courage, Coriolanus called off the attack.

he had turned on his country and family. "Let there be no doubt of this," she told him. "You shall never attack Rome unless you trample first upon the dead body of the mother who bore you." As a wave of shame washed over him, Coriolanus suddenly came to his senses. "You have saved Rome," he exclaimed. As he left her, he added, "But you have destroyed your son."[43]

Volumnia soon learned the meaning of those last words her son had spoken to her. A few hours later, he ordered the Volscian soldiers to retreat and then refused to command them anymore. Soon, the Volscian military campaign fell apart. When the Volscian king heard what had transpired, he had Coriolanus executed.

The Goddess and the Maiden

By counseling her son to do the right thing, Volumnia had saved Rome and allowed it to continue growing and expanding. In time, it came to control all of Italy. At the same time, its social customs, including its religious traditions, became increasingly sophisticated. The Roman faith had always been tolerant of others' beliefs. The proof for that had been the earlier avid borrowing of beliefs and myths from Greek religion. Similarly, for one reason or another Rome sometimes absorbed the gods of other nations and peoples into its own pantheon.

One of the most popular of those foreign deities was Cybele, a wise fertility and mother goddess from Anatolia (what is now Turkey). According to a popular myth, her entry into Rome's religion in the late 200s BCE was made possible by the bold, selfless efforts of another female hero—Claudia Quinta. Like other Romans, Claudia Quinta had heard that the chief priests had decided to welcome Cybele to Roman society. To that end, five Roman senators sailed across the sea to Anatolia and there found a black rock that was said to be sacred to the goddess. Their ship then brought the object back to Italy.

The plan was to take the rock down the Tiber River to Rome. But thanks to a recent drought, the water at the river's mouth was shallow and choked with mud. The vessel became trapped, and even the efforts of hundreds of soldiers pulling on ropes failed to free it. The senators saw this as a bad omen. Perhaps, they suggested, the existing Roman deities did not want Cybele to join their ranks.

Suddenly, however, out of the crowd of onlookers stepped young Claudia Quinta. Walking to the distraught senators, she offered to help, but they only laughed at the idea that a single, small woman could succeed when hundreds of Roman men could not.

Ovid later told how Claudia ignored these taunts and trudged through the mud to Cybele's black stone. "Kind and fruitful Mother," she said, "accept a suppliant's prayers."[44] The girl proceeded to offer to die if the goddess would finish the journey and join the other gods.

Seconds later Claudia pulled lightly on one of the ropes, and to the amazement of all present, the massive ship slipped free from the muck and glided straight to her. A few of the onlookers later claimed they saw Cybele herself step down from the vessel and onto Roman soil. Moreover, Claudia remained very much alive, which suggested that the goddess saw no reason for her to die. Once more, a brave and selfless woman had affected Rome's fortunes for the better. The names of other women like her were destined to echo through the extraordinarily long corridors of that nation's history. And anyone who might momentarily doubt that its many successes were the work of women and men alike needed only to glance at Rome's cherished collection of myths.

SOURCE NOTES

Introduction: A City Destined to Rule the World?

1. Quoted in Virgil, *Aeneid*, trans. Patric Dickinson. New York: New American Library, 2002, pp. 172–73.
2. Quoted in Virgil, *Aeneid*, p. 173.
3. Livy, *History of Rome from Its Foundation*, Books 1–5 published as *Livy: The Early History of Rome*, trans. Aubrey de Sélincourt. New York: Penguin, 2002, pp. 33–34.
4. Jane F. Gardner, *Roman Myths*. Austin: University of Texas Press, 1993, pp. 9, 41.

Chapter One: Rome's Many Borrowed Gods and Myths

5. Quoted in "Ovid, Fasti 1," Theoi Greek Mythology. www.theoi .com.
6. R.M. Ogilvie, *The Romans and Their Gods in the Age of Augustus*. New York: Norton, 1969, p. 11.
7. Sallust, *The War with Catiline*, trans. John C. Rolfe. Cambridge, MA: Harvard University Press, 1931, p. 99.
8. Gardner, *Roman Myths*, p. 78.

Chapter Two: Aeneas's Quest for a New Homeland

9. Michael Stapleton, *The Illustrated Dictionary of Greek and Roman Mythology*. New York: Bedrick, 1986, p. 14.
10. Gardner, *Roman Myths*, p. 10.
11. Gardner, *Roman Myths*, p. 9.
12. R.H. Barrow, *The Romans*. New York: Pelican, 1987, pp. 85–86.
13. Quoted in Virgil, *Aeneid*, p. 17.
14. Quoted in Virgil, *Aeneid*, p. 70.
15. Quoted in Virgil, *Aeneid*, p. 70.
16. Virgil, *Aeneid*, p. 1.
17. Norma L. Goodrich, *Ancient Myths*. New York: Plume, 1994, p. 250.
18. Quoted in Virgil, *Aeneid*, p. 11.

Chapter Three: Romulus Founds Rome, the Eternal City

19. Livy, *The Early History of Rome*, p. 37.
20. Livy, *The Early History of Rome*, p. 38.
21. Livy, *The Early History of Rome*, p. 39.
22. Gardner, *Roman Myths*, p. 16.
23. T.J. Cornell, *The Beginnings of Rome: Italy and Rome from the Bronze Age to the Punic Wars*. London: Routledge, 1995, p. 65.
24. Livy, *The Early History of Rome*, p. 40.
25. Livy, *The Early History of Rome*, p. 42.
26. Livy, *The Early History of Rome*, pp. 42–43.
27. Plutarch, *Romulus*, trans. John Dryden, Internet Classics Archive. http://classics.mit.edu.
28. Michael Grant, *History of Rome*. New York: Scribner's, 1997, pp. 55–56.

Chapter Four: Heroes Who Sacrificed All for Rome

29. Livy, *History of Rome from Its Foundation*. Books 6–10 published as *Rome and Italy*, trans. Betty Radice. New York: Penguin, 1982, p. 103.
30. Livy, *Rome and Italy*, p. 103.
31. Gardner, *Roman Myths*, p. 41.
32. Livy, *The Early History of Rome*, p. 116.
33. Quoted in Livy, *The Early History of Rome*, p. 118.
34. Quoted in Livy, *The Early History of Rome*, pp. 118–19.
35. Quoted in Livy, *The Early History of Rome*, p. 119.

Chapter Five: Brave, Patriotic Women of Rome's Past

36. Livy, *The Early History of Rome*, p. 231.
37. Livy, *The Early History of Rome*, pp. 234–35.
38. Quoted in Livy, *The Early History of Rome*, p. 236.
39. Mark Cartwright, "The Role of Women in the Roman World," World History Encyclopedia, February 22, 2014. www.worldhistory.org.
40. Gardner, *Roman Myths*, p. 53.
41. Livy, *The Early History of Rome*, p. 120.
42. Livy, *The Early History of Rome*, p. 120.
43. Quoted in Ian Scott-Kilvert, trans., *Plutarch: Makers of Rome*. New York: Penguin, 1988, pp. 48–49.
44. Quoted in Ovid, *Fasti, Book Four*, trans. A.S. Kline. Poetry in Translation, 2004. www.poetryintranslation.com.

FOR FURTHER RESEARCH

Books

E.M. Berens, *Myths and Legends of Ancient Greece and Rome*. London: Purple Unicorn, 2023.

Frank Edgar, *Greek and Roman Mythology*. Quincy, IL: Mark Twain Media, 2022.

William S. Fox, *Greek and Roman Mythology*. Whittier, CA: Creative Media, 2023.

Don Nardo, *Roman Mythology*. San Diego, CA: ReferencePoint, 2021.

Robert Stephan and John Sutherland, *Meet the Ancients: Gateway to Greece and Rome*. Bakersfield, CA: Argos, 2023.

Elara Vilar, *Adventures in Ancient Rome: Gods and Heroes*. Oxford, UK: Greener Planet 4us, 2023.

Internet Sources

Saugat Adhicari, "Top 10 Popular and Fascinating Myths in Ancient Rome," Ancient History Lists, September 2, 2022. www.ancienthistorylists.com.

Jona Lendering, "Gn. Marcius Coriolanus," Livius, October 4, 2020. www.livius.org.

Jona Lendering, "Janus," Livius, October 4, 2020. www.livius.org.

PBS, "The Roman Empire in the First Century: Mythology." www.pbs.org.

Plutarch, *Romulus*, trans. John Dryden, Internet Classics Archive. http://classics.mit.edu.

Theoi.com, "Roman Gods vs. Greeks Gods: Know the Difference," 2019. www.theoi.com.

Websites

The Classics Pages: Virgil's *Aeneid*
www.users.globalnet.co.uk/~loxias/aeneid1.htm
A simplified translation of Book 1 of Virgil's classic tale of Aeneas and the founding of the Roman race.

Heritage History

www.heritage-history.com/index.php?c=read&author=morris&book=roman&story=_front

Heritage History is an electronic library. From this page, users can access a PDF version of *Historical Tales: The Romance of Reality* by popular nineteenth-century novelist and journalist Charles Morris. The book contains numerous stories about ancient Rome, including several well-known Roman myths.

Mythopedia: Ultimate Guide to Roman Mythology

https://mythopedia.com/guides/roman-mythology

A team of scholars created and monitors this very useful site. It provides many separate, fulsome, accurate articles about the Roman gods, heroes, and myths.

United Nations of Roma Victrix (UNRV)

www.unrv.com

This site contains general descriptions of many aspects of ancient Roman life and customs, including government offices (of both the Republic and Empire); military armor and customs; gladiatorial games; slavery; and more.

World History Encyclopedia

www.worldhistory.org/Rome

Founded in 2009, this series of online articles endeavors to present the main highlights of world history concisely but accurately. It benefits from the writing talents of historians Joshua J. Mark and Mark Cartwright, along with their researchers and assistants. From the "Ancient Rome" page, readers can click on links to many articles about Roman history, culture, and mythology. Each article contains additional links to related topics.

INDEX

PICTURE CREDITS

Cover: Sergey Rusakov/Shutterstock

 6: Maury Aaseng
10: Alamy Stock Photo
13: Universal Images Group North America LLC/Alamy Stock Photo
15: Ivy Close Images/Alamy Stock Photo
20: Peter Horree/Alamy Stock Photo
23: Science History Images/Alamy Stock Photo
26: The Picture Art Collection/Alamy Stock Photo
30: Stocktrek Images, Inc./Alamy Stock Photo
33: Photo © Photo Josse / Bridgeman Images
36: Peter Horree/Alamy Stock Photo
40: The History Collection/Alamy Stock Photo
43: PAINTING/Alamy Stock Photo
45: Heritage Image Partnership Ltd/Alamy Stock Photo
49: Peter Horree/Alamy Stock Photo
52: ARTGEN/Alamy Stock Photo
54: Thunderstruck/Alamy Stock Photo

ABOUT THE AUTHOR

Classical historian and award-winning author Don Nardo has written numerous acclaimed volumes about ancient civilizations and peoples. They include more than fifty overviews of the mythologies of the Sumerians, Babylonians, Egyptians, Greeks, Romans, Persians, Celts, Hindus, Native Americans, and others. Nardo, who also composes and arranges orchestral music, lives with his wife, Christine, in Massachusetts.